THE NIGHT BEFORE TOUCH-A-TRUCK

WRITTEN BY: STACEY CHENEY

ILLUSTRATED BY: TESS CASTELLA

FOR MYLES AND NOAH

It was the night before Touch-a-Truck,
and all through the town,
all the big trucks were prepping
and whizzing around.

The fire trucks were polished,
looking shiny and new.
And the others were primping,
getting washed and waxed, too!

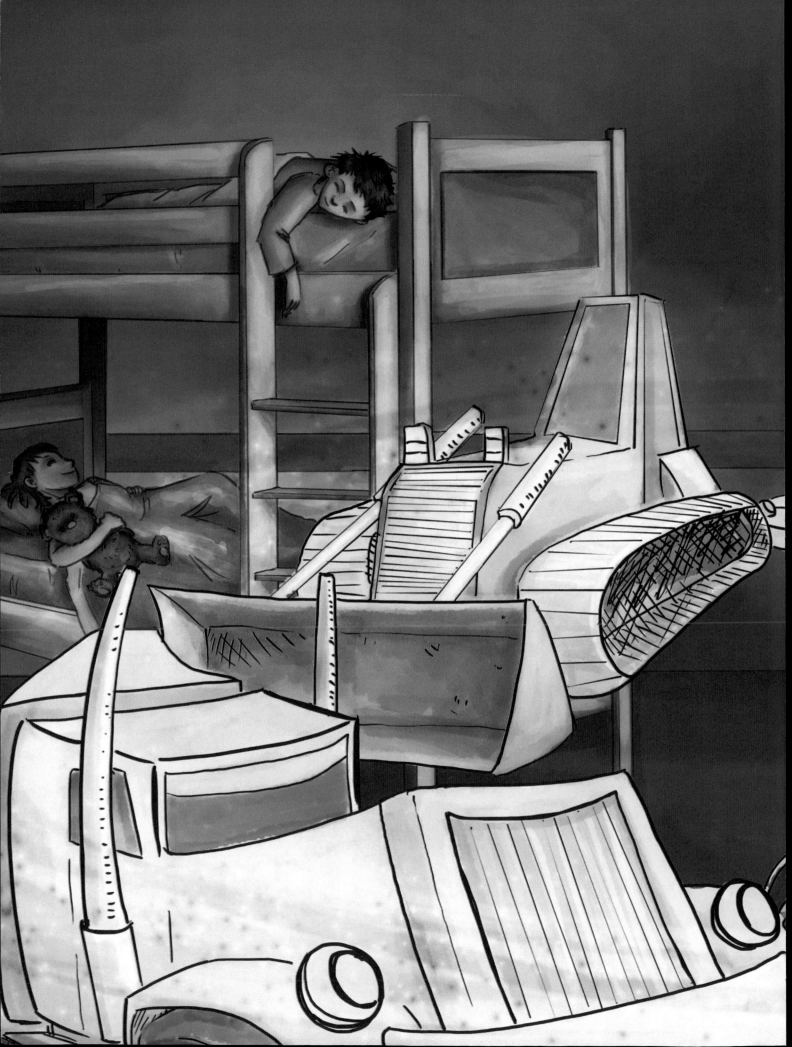

The children were nestled all snug in their beds,
while visions of tanker trucks

zoomed through their heads.

They dreamed of huge tractors and box trucks galore.
They dreamed of bulldozers and buses and more!

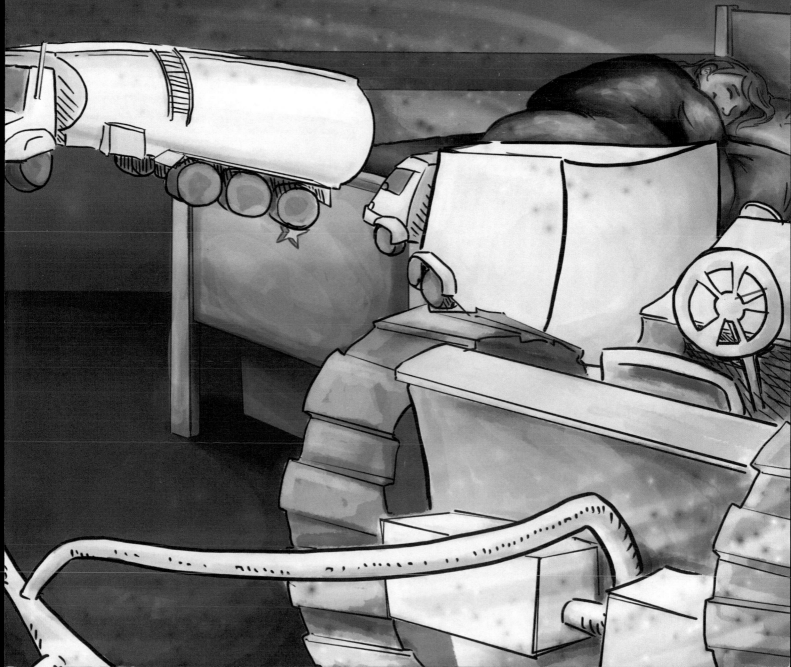

While out on the street was a sight to behold -

All kinds of big trucks - red, blue, green, and gold!

They slowly pulled in, and went right to their places.

The thrill of the night showed on everyone's faces.

The moon on the blacktop of the town parking lot
made it look like a disco - a funky, cool spot.

When all of a sudden, there came such a sound.
And wouldn't you know, those trucks began to get down!

With dance moves so nimble, so lively, so hearty,

it was clear in an instant it was one big dance party.

Cooler than cats, those big trucks, they grooved.

And they beeped, and they honked, and they sang while they moved.

"I'm Mixer! I'm Digger!

I'm Dumper! I'm Paver!

I'm Mover! I'm Dozer!

I'm a Big Excavator!

We're all here together!
Now hear our call!
And dance away! Dance away!

Dance away all!"

And then, in a flash, they began to prepare

for the company of children soon to be there -

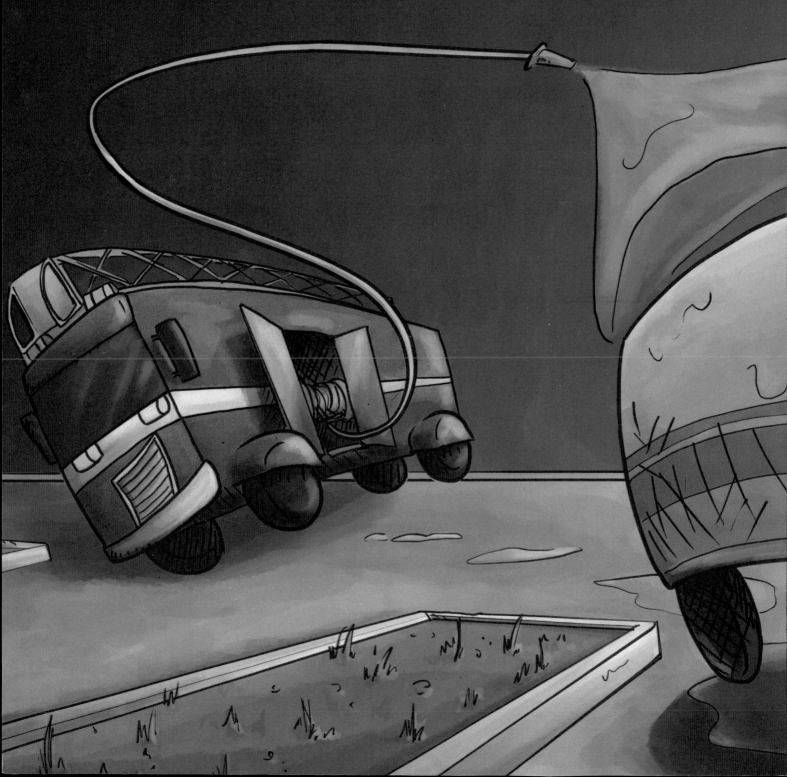

Children who laugh and discover and play,

who have waited so long to enjoy Touch-a-Truck Day.

The children, who will sit and will ride and will steer,
who will wave at their friends
while they scream and they cheer.

It's all the trucks think of,
it's all that they crave -

To bring joy to the boys and the girls who behave.

The trucks, how they glistened!

Their wheels, so shiny!

All lined up in a row,

and not one of them tiny!

Their loud, noisy horns

were ready to blow.

Their engines were revving

and ready to go!

The garbage truck sprayed
his best garbage cologne,

And up went the ladder,
for which Fire Truck's known.

The tractor got muddy
to make it feel real,

And the big concrete mixer
spun around like a wheel.

By the time the sun rose,
      the big day was here -

                  The trucks' and the children's
                        best day of the year!

In came the crowds of large families and neighbors,

and the trucks finally saw the fruits of their labors.

When the day ended,

the team started packing.

To get to their next job,

they need to get cracking.

But I heard them exclaim,

as they drove out of sight:

"Happy Touch-a-Truck Day to all!
And to all a good night!"

Made in the USA
Lexington, KY
27 April 2016